I AM BEAR

For Rhi, Gee, Kit and Harv.
And Siobhan, always.
B.B.S.

For Mini, Reisy and B.
S.A.

First published 2016 by Walker Entertainment, an imprint of Walker Books Ltd

87 Vauxhall Walk, London SE11 5HJ

2 4 6 8 10 9 7 5 3 1

Text © 2016 Ben Bailey Smith

Illustrations © 2016 Sav Akyüz

The right of Ben Bailey Smith and Sav Akyüz to be identified as author and illustrator respectively
of this work has been asserted by them in accordance with the Copyright, Designs and Patents Act 1988.

This book has been typeset in Bokka Solid.

Printed in Malaysia

British Library Cataloguing in Publication Data:

a catalogue record for this book is available from the British Library

ISBN 978-1-4063-5925-1

www.walker.co.uk

I AM BEAR

Ben Bailey Smith

and

Sav Akyüz

WALKER
ENTERTAINMENT

I am Bear.

And I am bare.

The suit I wear

has purple hair.

In my tummy?
Mostly honey.

Here's a thingy
I find funny...

Knock!
Knock!

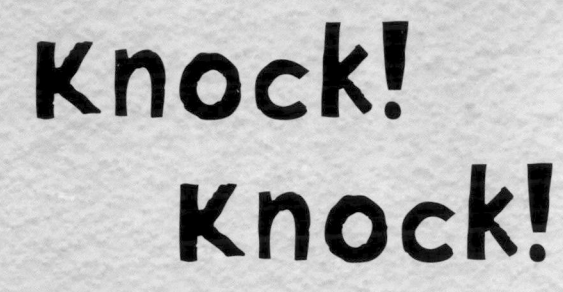

who's there?

Munch,
munch.

My lunch.

I do magic.

Most bears won't.

Now you see me...

Now you don't!

Look behind you.

Cops and robbers!
That's my favourite.

Guess who ate it?

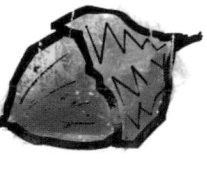
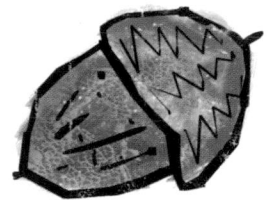

Fun with friends,
that's the main thing.

Favourite hobby?

Probably painting.

I am Bear,
and I was there...

Now I'm gone...